This storybook belongs to:

....

LADYBIRD

Favourite
Fairy Tales
FOR
GIRLS

Retold by Mandy Archer
Cover illustrated by Estelle Corke

A catalogue record for this book is available from the British Library

Published by Ladybird Books Ltd
80 Strand, London, WC2R 0RL
A Penguin Company

002-2 4 6 8 10 9 7 5 3
© LADYBIRD BOOKS LTD MMXI
LADYBIRD and the device of a Ladybird are trademarks of Ladybird Books Ltd

ISBN: 978-1-40930-876-8

Printed in China

LADYBIRD

FAVOURITE
FAIRY TALES
FOR
GIRLS

Contents

CINDERELLA

An ancient tale about a beautiful girl who enchants a handsome prince. When Cinderella's fairy godmother waves her wand, anything can happen.

LITTLE RED RIDING HOOD

A classic fairy tale set in a shady forest. Can sweet Little Red Riding Hood escape the wolf who poses as her grandmother?

HANSEL
AND GRETEL

A story showing the unbreakable bond between a brother and his sister. When Hansel and Gretel meet a witch, only their quick wits can save them.

THE MAGIC
PORRIDGE POT

A folk tale about a poor village girl who is given a magic porridge pot. She only has to say the right words and her pot will cook and cook and cook.

SLEEPING BEAUTY

*An ancient story about a
princess who falls into an enchanted
slumber. Can Sleeping Beauty's true love
find his way to her spellbound castle?*

LITTLE RED HEN

*A fable for the lazy and the
hard-hearted. When Little Red Hen
decides to make a loaf of bread, not one
of her friends is willing to help her.*

GOLDILOCKS AND THE THREE BEARS

A well-loved tale about a girl who is too bold for her own good. Goldilocks is so curious about the three bears' cottage, she can't help tiptoeing inside.

THE UGLY DUCKLING

A fairy story about a lonely little bird with a big heart. The Ugly Duckling's journey reveals that true beauty hides deep inside all of us.

CINDERELLA

Based on an original story by Charles Perrault, although the earliest tales of a girl like Cinderella come from Ancient Egypt

Illustrated by Marina Le Ray

ONCE UPON A TIME there was
a beautiful young girl called
Cinderella. She lived in a small cottage
with her stepmother and two stepsisters.
Even though Cinderella was gentle and
kind, the stepsisters and their mother
treated her cruelly.

Every morning, Cinderella had to do all the housework.
While she scrubbed, cleaned, tidied and cooked, her stepmother
and stepsisters sat eating cake and drinking tea.

One day, the stepsisters were very excited. The prince of the kingdom had invited them to attend a special ball at the royal palace!

"Am I invited, too?" Cinderella asked in a tiny voice.

The stepsisters both shook their heads.

"How can you come?" screeched the first stepsister. "Your dress is stitched out of rags."

The second stepsister pointed at Cinderella's bare feet. "Look! You don't even have any shoes to wear."

Cinderella stared sadly down at her careworn clothes. She didn't have the lovely gowns her stepsisters did.

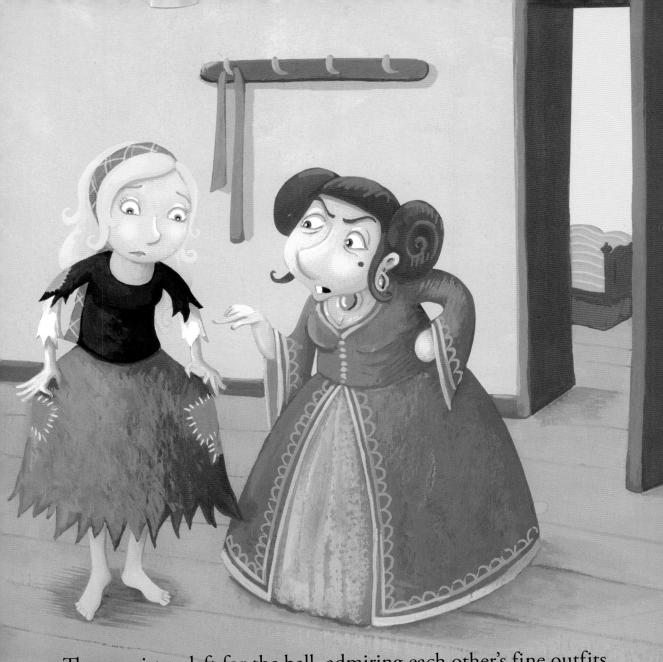

The stepsisters left for the ball, admiring each other's fine outfits.
"The prince is sure to want to marry one of us!" they cackled.

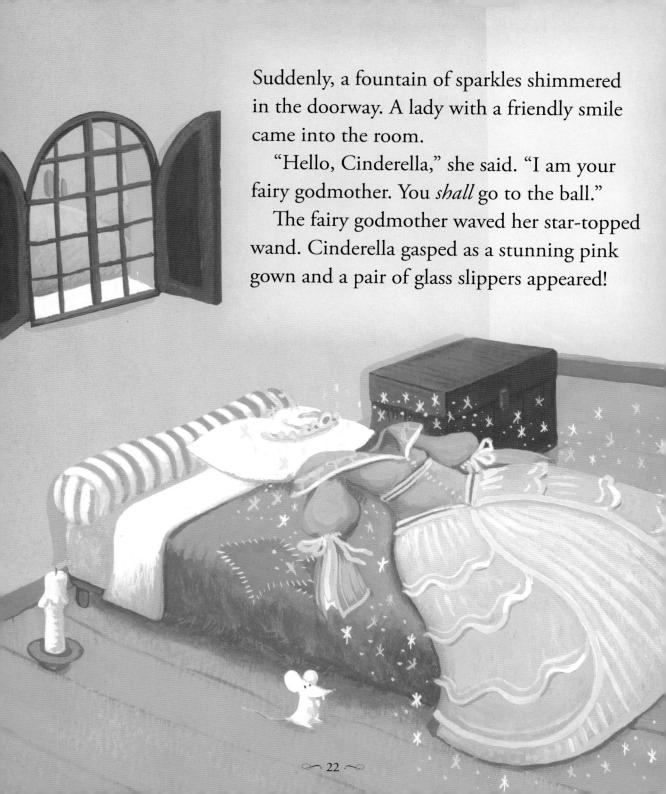

Suddenly, a fountain of sparkles shimmered in the doorway. A lady with a friendly smile came into the room.

"Hello, Cinderella," she said. "I am your fairy godmother. You *shall* go to the ball."

The fairy godmother waved her star-topped wand. Cinderella gasped as a stunning pink gown and a pair of glass slippers appeared!

Cinderella quickly got dressed. The pink gown and delicate glass slippers fitted perfectly!

The fairy godmother led the girl out to the front garden. She pointed her magic wand at a pumpkin and then at two mice playing in the grass. In an instant the pumpkin was transformed into a beautiful coach. The mice became majestic white horses.

Cinderella got ready to leave.

"Make sure you're home before the last chime of midnight," warned the fairy godmother. "That's when the spell will break."

When Cinderella arrived at the palace, no one recognized her in such fine clothes. Everyone was talking about the mysterious, beautiful girl in the pink dress.

The prince was enchanted from the very first moment that he saw Cinderella.

"May I have this dance?" he asked, twirling her round and round the ballroom.

It was the most wonderful evening of Cinderella's life. The prince danced only with her until the clock struck twelve. Cinderella gasped when she heard the chimes.

"It's midnight!" she whispered. "I have to leave."

Cinderella left the palace ballroom as fast as she could.

"Come back!" begged the prince. "I don't even know your name."

The poor girl knew she couldn't stop – the magic was going to disappear at any moment!

In her rush to leave, Cinderella lost one of her glass slippers on the staircase.

The prince watched her go, clutching the shoe in his hand.

Cinderella ran home as fast as she could. By the time she crept into bed, her dress had become rags once more.

The prince travelled the kingdom searching for the stranger who had captured his heart.

"I will marry the girl whose foot fits this slipper," he announced.

One day, he and his footman turned into the lane where Cinderella lived.

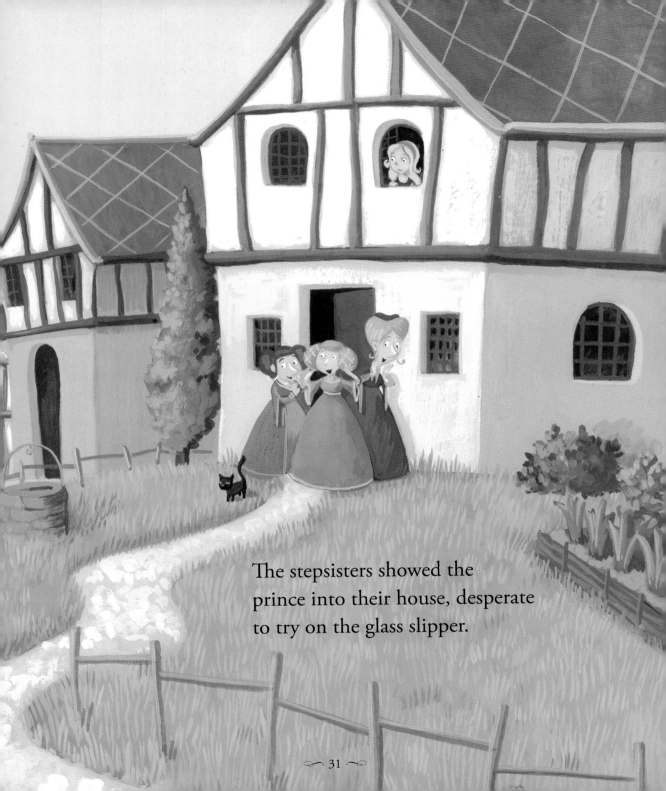

The stepsisters showed the
prince into their house, desperate
to try on the glass slipper.

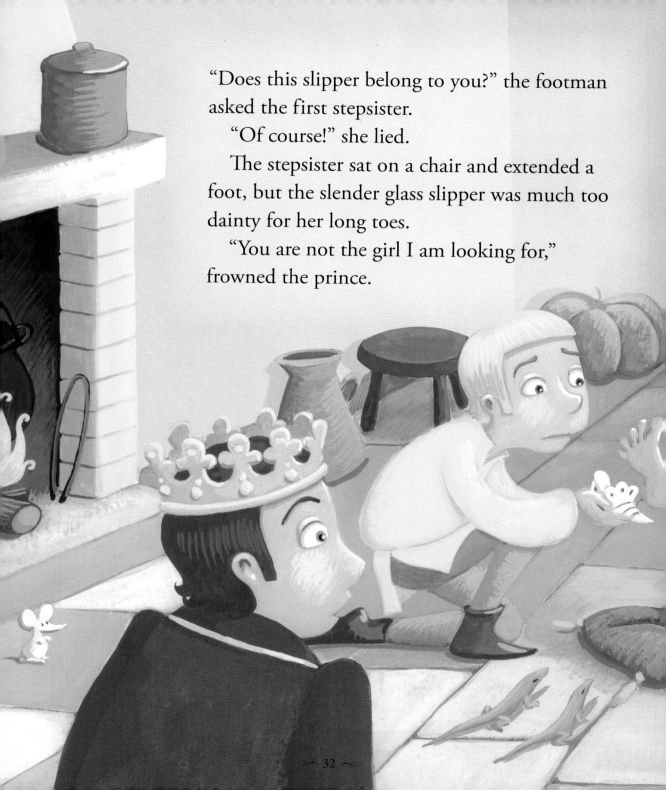

"Does this slipper belong to you?" the footman asked the first stepsister.

"Of course!" she lied.

The stepsister sat on a chair and extended a foot, but the slender glass slipper was much too dainty for her long toes.

"You are not the girl I am looking for," frowned the prince.

Cinderella watched nervously
in the background.

The second stepsister pushed herself in front of the prince.

"It must be me, sire!" she grinned.

She tried and tried to wedge her toes into the shoe, but it was hopeless. The slipper was much too small for her chubby foot.

"Is there anyone else?" asked the prince.

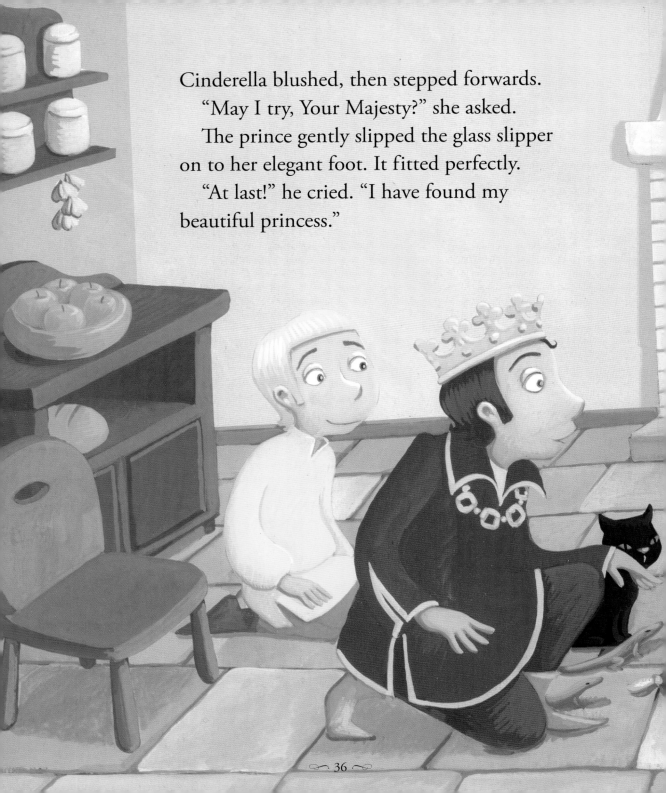

Cinderella blushed, then stepped forwards.
"May I try, Your Majesty?" she asked.
The prince gently slipped the glass slipper
on to her elegant foot. It fitted perfectly.
"At last!" he cried. "I have found my
beautiful princess."

The prince didn't care about Cinderella's rags. Instead he saw the enchanting girl who had won his heart in the palace ballroom.

"Will you marry me?" he asked.

Cinderella agreed at once. The prince immediately whisked her away to the palace, where they lived happily ever after.

LITTLE RED RIDING HOOD

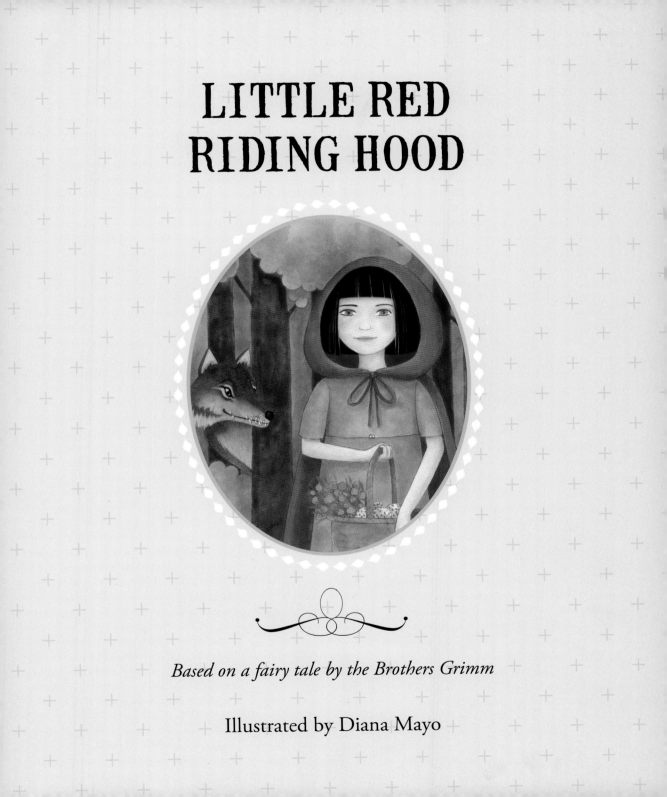

Based on a fairy tale by the Brothers Grimm

Illustrated by Diana Mayo

ONCE UPON A TIME, there was
a young girl who lived with her mother
and father in a little house at the edge
of the forest. She was known as
Little Red Riding Hood because she
loved to wear a beautiful cloak
made out of scarlet velvet.

One morning, Little Red Riding Hood's mother had a special errand for her.

"Your grandmother is ill," she explained. "Please take her this basket of cakes."

"Of course!" smiled Little Red Riding Hood. She decided to set off straight away.

Little Red Riding Hood's grandmother lived on the far side of the forest. The walk was dark and lonely, but Little Red Riding Hood had made the journey many times before.

"Make sure that you stay on the path," said her father, waving goodbye.

Her mother gave her a kiss. "And say a polite good morning to Grandmother."

"I will," nodded Little Red Riding Hood.

Little Red Riding Hood's mother and father did not know that a wolf lived in the forest. He was a fierce old beast with sharp teeth and cunning yellow eyes. The wolf sniffed the air. He was feeling especially hungry today.

As she walked along the path,
Little Red Riding Hood sang a
song to herself. She didn't spot
the wolf listening from behind a
tree, his yellow eyes blazing.

"She'll make a fine supper!"
he decided.

The wolf crept out of sight, then dashed through the trees as fast as his legs could carry him. He didn't stop running until he reached the cottage where Little Red Riding Hood's grandmother lived. The wolf knocked gently on the front door.

"Come in," called a weak voice.

The wolf burst into the room. Quick as a flash, he rolled the old woman up in a rug and hid her under the bed. He quickly put on her nightgown and bonnet.

A while later Little Red Riding Hood skipped up the path, eager to see her beloved grandmother. She knocked on the front door.

"Come in!" called a gruff voice.

Little Red Riding Hood's heart fluttered. Her grandmother sounded very strange today!

Little Red Riding Hood stepped nervously into her grandmother's cottage. She could see the old lady sitting up in bed, knitting a pair of socks, but something about her seemed funny.

"Come closer, my dear," said the wolf, trying to make his voice sound reedy and soft.

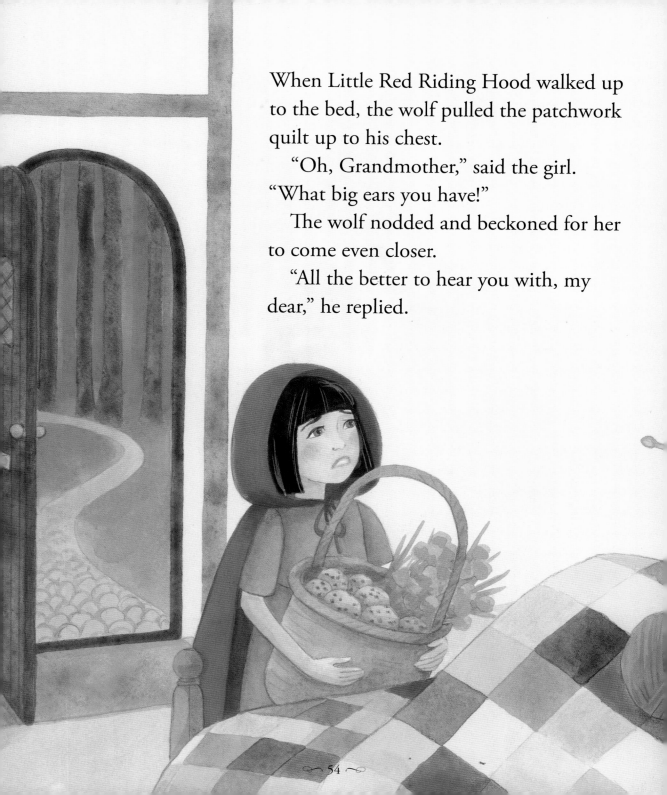

When Little Red Riding Hood walked up to the bed, the wolf pulled the patchwork quilt up to his chest.

"Oh, Grandmother," said the girl. "What big ears you have!"

The wolf nodded and beckoned for her to come even closer.

"All the better to hear you with, my dear," he replied.

Little Red Riding Hood stepped forward and gazed into the wolf's face. The sly creature pulled the pink bonnet down a little lower.

"Oh, Grandmother," said the girl. "What big eyes you have!"

The wolf couldn't help licking his lips.

"All the better to see you with, my dear," he agreed.

Having Little Red Riding Hood so close made the wolf feel hungrier than ever. He smiled a broad smile, then got ready to pounce.

"Oh, Grandmother," said Little Red Riding Hood. "What big teeth you have!"

The wolf pulled back the covers and sprang out of bed.

"All the better to eat you with, my dear!" he snarled.

"Help!" screamed Little Red Riding Hood, running for the door. Her poor grandmother could only watch and tremble, still trapped under the bed.

The wolf flashed his claws and bared his teeth, almost tearing the girl's velvet cloak.

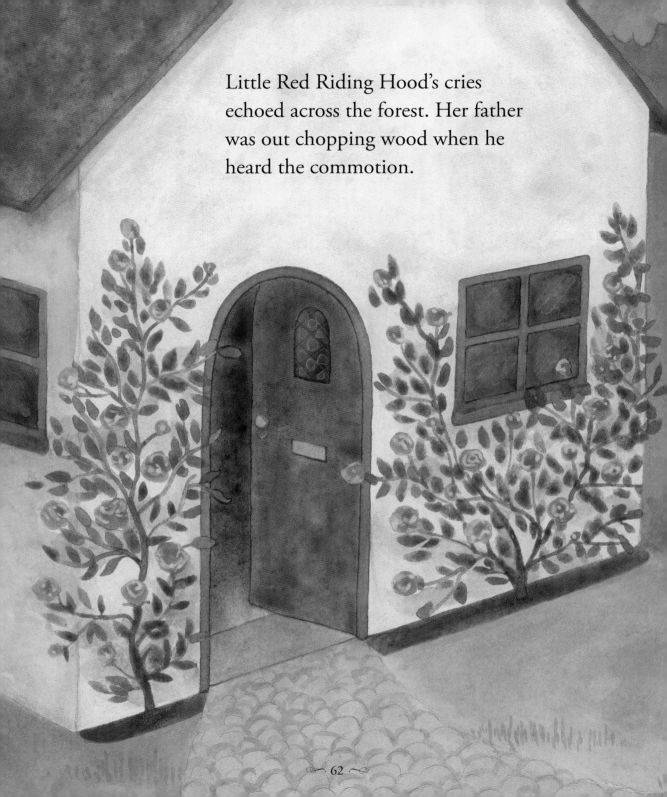

Little Red Riding Hood's cries
echoed across the forest. Her father
was out chopping wood when he
heard the commotion.

Little Red Riding Hood's father snatched up his heavy axe. He ran all the way to Grandmother's cottage and stormed inside.

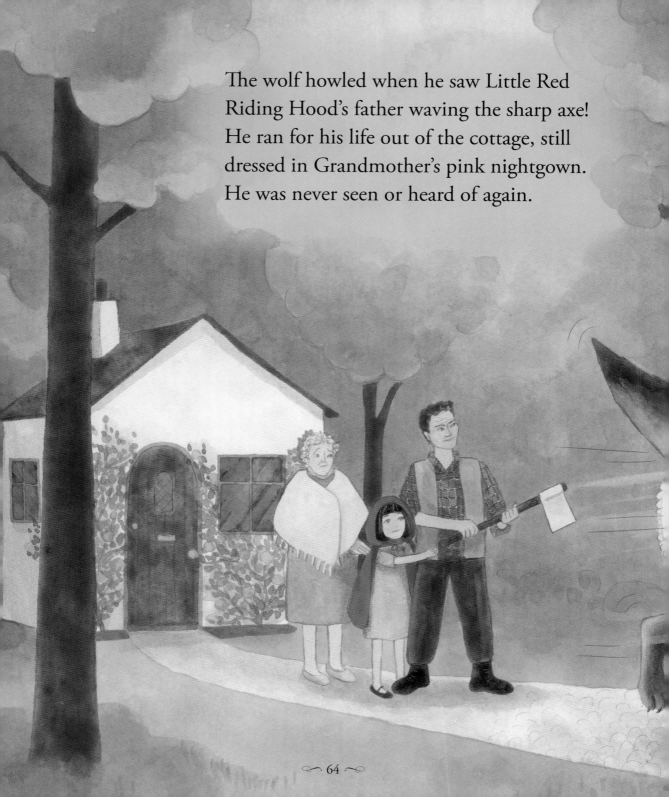

The wolf howled when he saw Little Red
Riding Hood's father waving the sharp axe!
He ran for his life out of the cottage, still
dressed in Grandmother's pink nightgown.
He was never seen or heard of again.

HANSEL
AND GRETEL

Based on a fairy tale by the Brothers Grimm

Illustrated by Marina Le Ray

A LONG TIME AGO, two children lived in a forest with their father and stepmother. Hansel and Gretel were both helpful and kind, but times were hard. Their father was a poor woodcutter who struggled to provide for his family. On many nights Hansel and Gretel had to go to bed without any supper.

The family got poorer and poorer until one day the few coins they had ran out.

"We cannot feed four mouths," snapped the stepmother. "The children must go."

The woodcutter begged his wife to change her mind, but she wouldn't give in. Hansel and Gretel listened at the door as their stepmother plotted to abandon them in the forest.

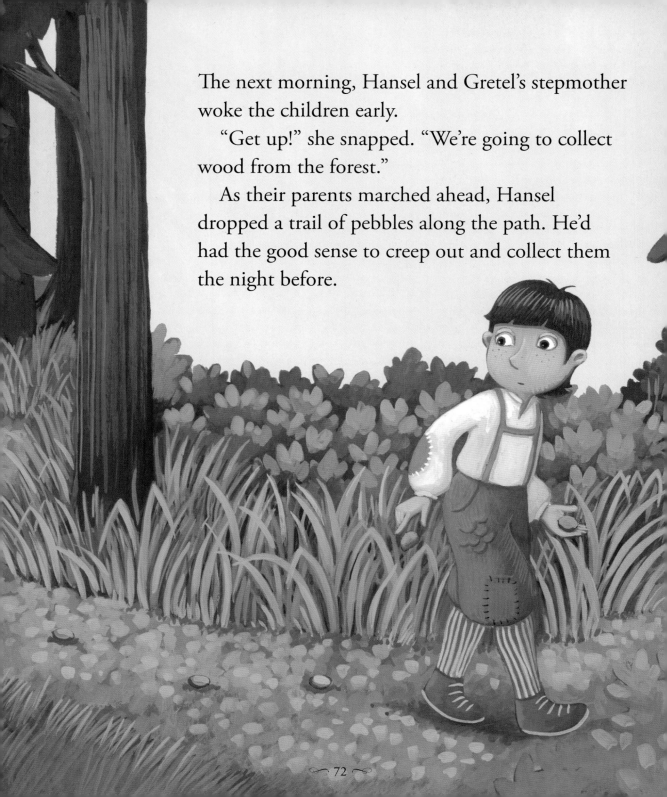

The next morning, Hansel and Gretel's stepmother
woke the children early.

"Get up!" she snapped. "We're going to collect
wood from the forest."

As their parents marched ahead, Hansel
dropped a trail of pebbles along the path. He'd
had the good sense to creep out and collect them
the night before.

When they reached the darkest part of the forest, Hansel and Gretel's father hugged them tightly.

"Wait here until we've finished chopping wood," he said.

The children waited until it got dark, but their father and stepmother didn't return.

"I'm frightened," wept Gretel.

Hansel pointed to the path and smiled. A line of pebbles shone in the silver moonlight.

Hansel and Gretel followed the trail of pebbles all the way back to their cottage.

"Thank heavens you're alive!" cried their father as he opened the door.

His wife stormed back to bed, her furious face twisted in the candlelight.

"We should have led them deeper into the forest," she whispered. "Next time they must never find their way home."

That night Hansel and Gretel's cruel stepmother locked them in their room so they couldn't pick up any more pebbles. As soon as it was daylight, they were taken back into the forest.

Hansel reached into his pocket and pulled out the crust of bread that he'd been given for breakfast. This time he secretly dropped crumbs along the path instead.

The woodcutter looked sad and tired when it was time to say goodbye.

"What shall we do now?" asked Gretel, watching her parents walk away.

"Look for the trail of breadcrumbs," smiled Hansel.

The little girl looked, but there was nothing there. The birds of the forest had eaten up every crumb.

The children walked helplessly through the trees. Suddenly they found themselves in a grassy clearing. There before them was a magical gingerbread house. The door was made of toffee and lollipop flowers dotted the garden. Hansel and Gretel couldn't resist eating a little. Every mouthful was delicious!

"Come in!" cried a little old lady sitting at the window.

As soon as Hansel and Gretel stepped inside, the old lady slammed the door behind them. She was a wicked witch who liked to eat lost little boys and girls.

"Get in here!" she snapped, bundling Hansel into an iron cage. "You'll make a delicious supper!"

The witch dragged Gretel to the kitchen.

"Open the oven door," she snarled. "You'll bake the bread to go with my feast."

Gretel could see that the old crone wanted to cook her, too.

"The oven isn't big enough," she pretended. "How will the bread tray fit in?"

The evil witch hobbled over and flung open the oven door. Flames curled and spat at the pair.

"Look, foolish girl!" she sneered. "It's even big enough for me to fit inside."

Gretel pretended to look. Then, with a great heave, she pushed the witch inside and shut the door.

Gretel unlocked Hansel's cage as fast as she could.

As her brother climbed out, something gleamed on the shelf beside Gretel. The little girl lifted down a chest filled with gold coins.

"We can buy food at last!" cried Hansel.

It took Hansel and Gretel a long time to make their way home. When they finally found the path back to their cottage, their father held his arms out with joy.

"Your stepmother has gone," he explained. "We'll never be parted again."

So the family lived happily ever after in their quiet cottage, surrounded by love and laughter.

THE MAGIC PORRIDGE POT

Based on a fairy tale by the Brothers Grimm

Illustrated by Laura Barella

ONCE UPON A TIME there was a young girl who lived with her mother. They were very poor and never had enough food to eat.

One day the little girl was so hungry she went out for a walk, hoping to find a few nuts and berries. In the woods she came across an old lady carrying a cooking pot.

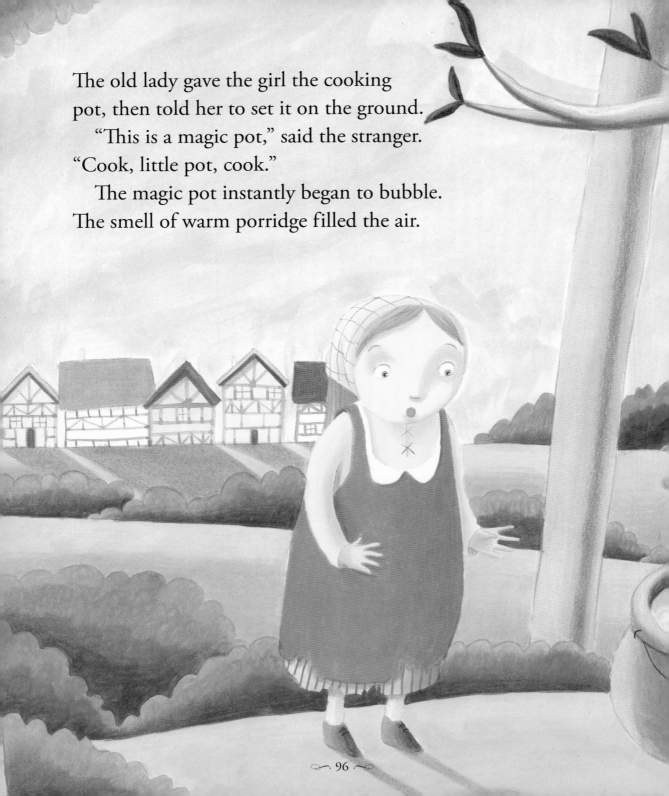

The old lady gave the girl the cooking pot, then told her to set it on the ground.

"This is a magic pot," said the stranger. "Cook, little pot, cook."

The magic pot instantly began to bubble. The smell of warm porridge filled the air.

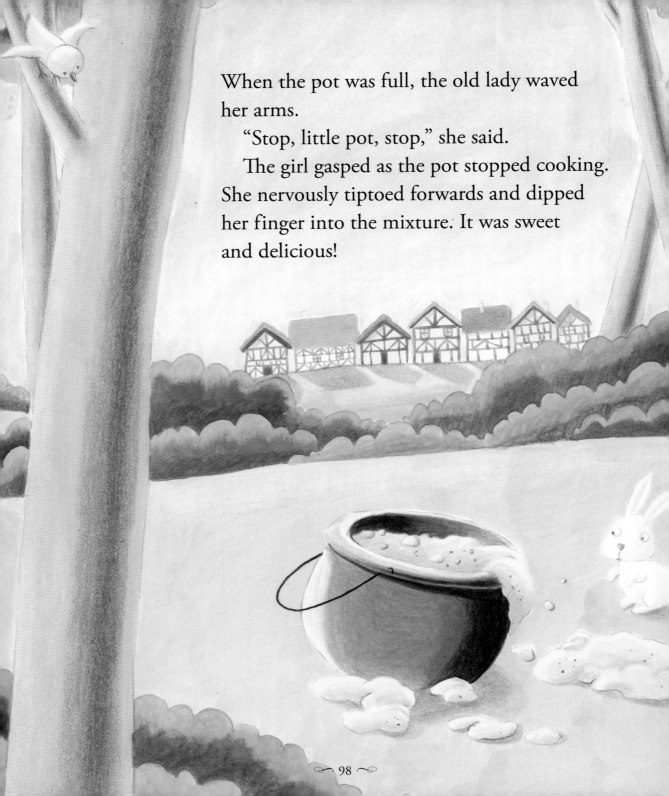

When the pot was full, the old lady waved
her arms.

"Stop, little pot, stop," she said.

The girl gasped as the pot stopped cooking.
She nervously tiptoed forwards and dipped
her finger into the mixture. It was sweet
and delicious!

The girl thanked the old lady and ran back to the village.
She burst into her kitchen and put the magic porridge pot
on the table.

"Our worries are over, Mother!" she cried. "Cook, little
pot, cook."

Her mother watched in astonishment as bubbles of sweet,
creamy porridge suddenly appeared in the magic porridge pot.

When there was enough the girl simply said, "Stop, little
pot, stop."

From that day onwards, the girl and her mother always
had more than enough food to eat. The mouth-watering bowls
of porridge made them grow healthy and strong. They only
had to say the magic words and their meal would be ready
in a trice.

Every day the pair said a little prayer of thanks for the
mysterious old lady and her generous gift.

One day, the girl had to run an errand in the next village. Her mother waved goodbye, then asked the magic pot to make some porridge for lunch.

"Cook, little pot, cook," she smiled.

The girl's mother ate her fill of porridge. The delicious lunch made her sleepy.

"I'll just sit for a while in my rocking chair," she decided.

Within moments, the woman had fallen asleep. While she dozed, the magic pot kept on bubbling. She had forgotten to tell it to stop!

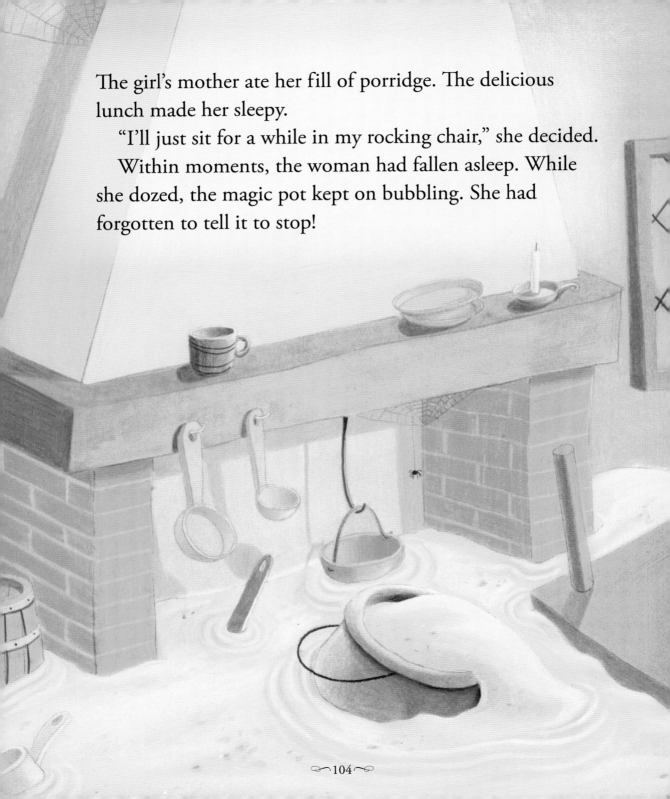

Soon golden porridge filled the cottage and oozed out
of the door.

With no one to tell it to stop, the pot kept on working its magic. The woman snored peacefully as porridge bubbled higher and higher!

Soon the mixture filled the kitchen. The rocking chair was carried out of the cottage in a swell of creamy porridge.

The woman slept and slept. Her rocking chair floated out of the cottage, down the lane and into the village streets. The magic cooking pot bobbed up and down, churning out more and more porridge.

"What is happening?" shouted the villagers.

The girl was still far away, so there was no one to tell the pot to stop. Women leant out of the balconies, children cried for help and men waded through the clogged streets.

The woman's cat leapt off her lap, but still she didn't wake up.

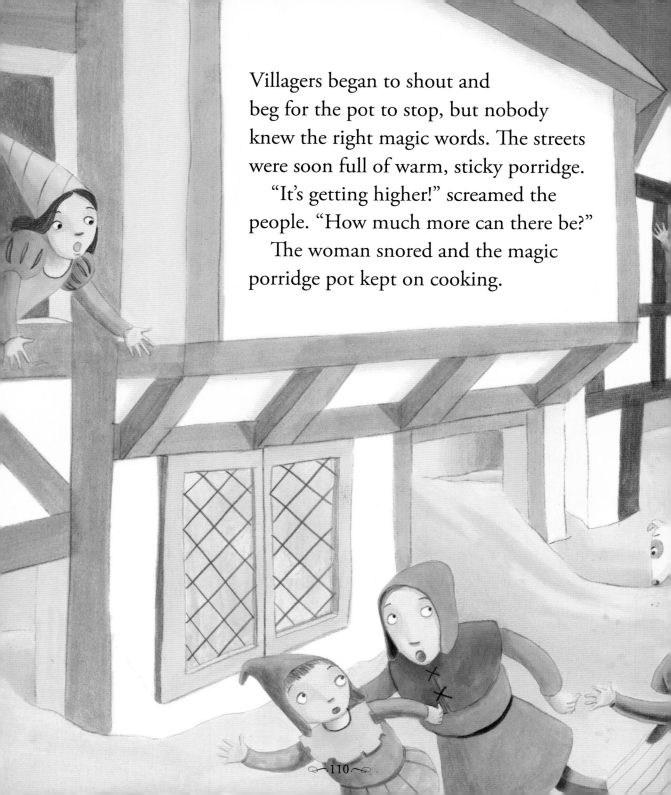

Villagers began to shout and beg for the pot to stop, but nobody knew the right magic words. The streets were soon full of warm, sticky porridge.

"It's getting higher!" screamed the people. "How much more can there be?"

The woman snored and the magic porridge pot kept on cooking.

When the girl got back to her village she was in for a terrible shock. The whole place was covered in a sea of creamy porridge. It even spilled out of the streets and up the lane towards her.

"It must be my magic porridge pot!" she exclaimed. "Whatever has happened to it?"

The girl shouted at the top of her voice.

"Stop, little pot, stop!"

The magic porridge pot stopped cooking as quickly as it had begun.

The girl's mother woke up with a start, unable to believe her eyes.

Now the flood had stopped, the villagers cheered. There was enough delicious porridge to feed everyone for months!

SLEEPING
BEAUTY

Based on an old French fairy tale

Illustrated by Richard Johnson

THERE WAS ONCE a king and a queen who longed for a child. After many years, the queen gave birth to a baby girl. The royal couple were so enchanted with their daughter, they invited all the good fairies in the land to become her godmothers.

On the day of her christening, the fairies gathered in the nursery.

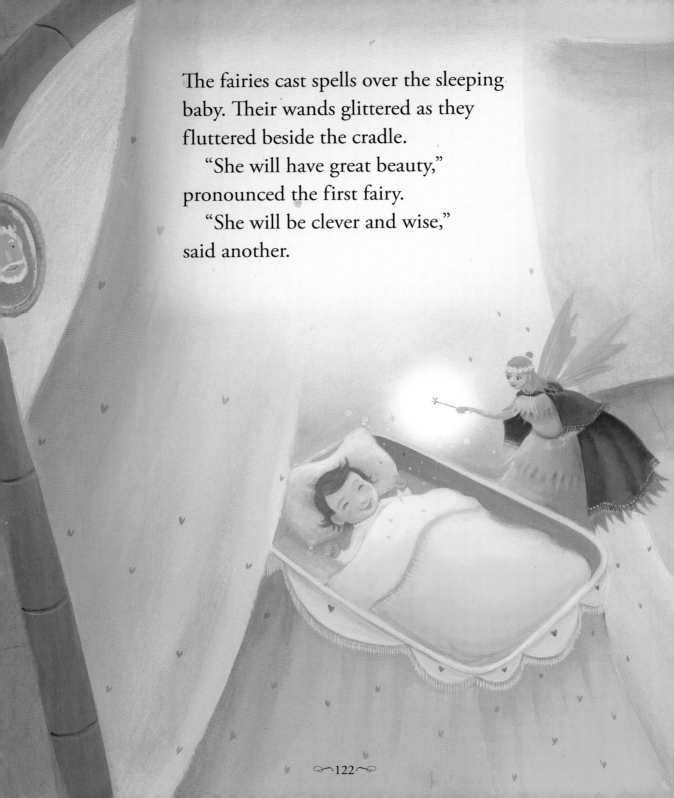

The fairies cast spells over the sleeping baby. Their wands glittered as they fluttered beside the cradle.

"She will have great beauty," pronounced the first fairy.

"She will be clever and wise," said another.

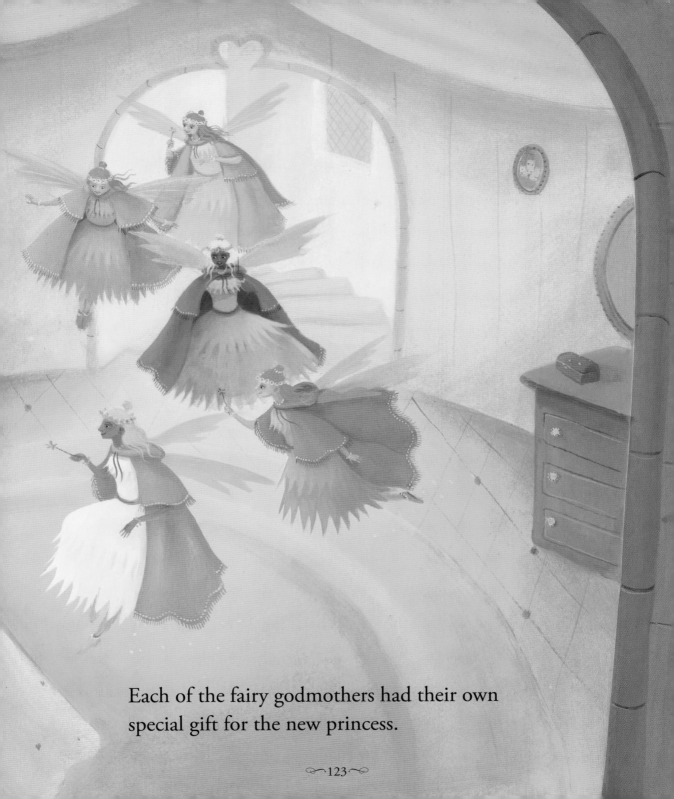

Each of the fairy godmothers had their own special gift for the new princess.

Just when the king and queen thought that
their joy was complete, another fairy appeared
at the castle window.

"Why was I not invited here today?"
she demanded.

The king and queen gasped. They had forgotten
that this fairy still lived in the kingdom!

The forgotten fairy was evil. Her green eyes flashed as she darted towards the cradle.

"I have a spell for the princess, too," she hissed. "In sixteen years she will prick her finger on a spinning wheel and die!"

The bad fairy cackled with laughter, then disappeared out of the window. The little princess began to cry.

"What are we to do?" asked the queen, cradling the baby to her chest.

"We must burn every spinning wheel in the land!" the king ordered.

None of the good fairies possessed magic strong enough to break the curse. There was, however, one glimmer of hope.

"I have yet to give my christening spell," said a fairy with golden wings.

A cascade of stardust burst from her tiny wand.

"The princess will not die," she said. "Instead she will prick her finger and fall asleep for one hundred years."

The fairy revealed that only a kiss of true love would be able to rouse the princess from her slumber.

The years passed. The king and queen's beloved daughter grew up to be just as enchanting as the good fairies had promised she would be.

She spent her days roaming the castle and its grounds, singing to the birds and animals.

Everybody adored the princess's kind heart and sweet ways.

One day, the princess discovered a staircase that she had never seen before.

"What could be up here?" she wondered.

A forgotten spinning wheel stood in the chamber at the top. When the princess reached out to touch it, the needle pricked her finger. She fell asleep straight away.

At the very same instant that the princess cut
her finger, every man, woman and child in
the kingdom fell into a deep slumber. Even
the animals fell asleep.

The castle slept like that for many years.
After a time, thorns and brambles grew
all over the stone building, hiding it from view.

The story of the mysterious Sleeping Beauty spread far and wide. Many brave knights tried to ride through the briars that covered the castle, but the thorns were too sharp to hack away.

One hundred years went by.

One day a noble prince passed the princess's tower.

"I shall break the fairy's curse," he promised.

The prince had been dreaming of meeting a beautiful princess for a long time. When he raised his sword, the briars parted before him.

He walked through the deserted courtyard and into the silent castle. All around servants, jesters and villagers lay where they'd fallen asleep one hundred years earlier.

The brave prince climbed the briars all the way up to the top of the tallest turret. He peered in the window and gasped.

"She is even more beautiful than I imagined," he whispered.

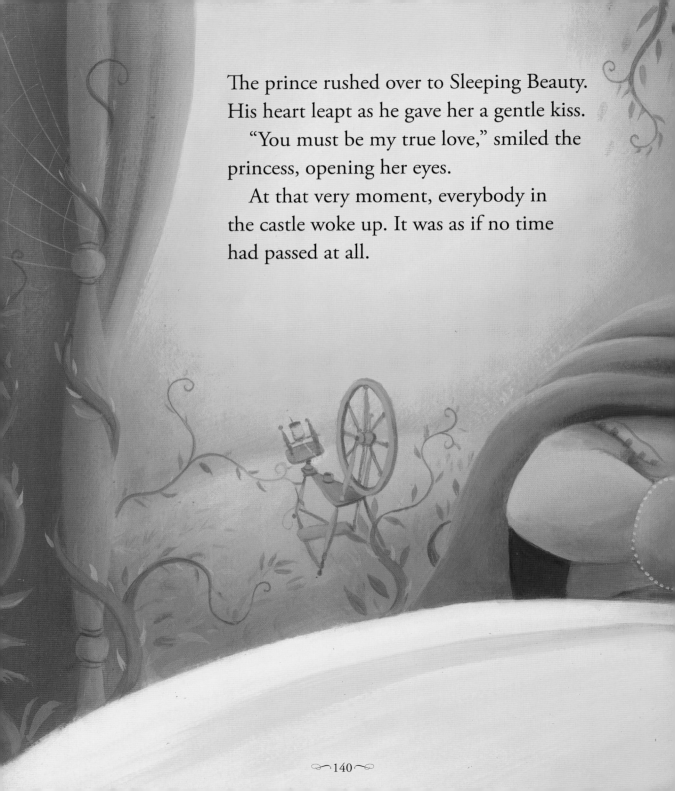

The prince rushed over to Sleeping Beauty. His heart leapt as he gave her a gentle kiss.

"You must be my true love," smiled the princess, opening her eyes.

At that very moment, everybody in the castle woke up. It was as if no time had passed at all.

The prince and princess were married the very next day. The kingdom rang with bells and dancing filled the streets. All of the good fairies came to join in the celebrations.

The bad fairy was furious when she heard that her curse was broken. She disappeared, leaving the prince and Sleeping Beauty to live happily ever after.

LITTLE
RED HEN

Based on an old English folk tale

Illustrated by Virginia Allyn

LITTLE RED HEN LIVED in a cosy farmhouse in the country. She shared it with an idle dog, a lazy cat and a sleepy little rat.

"Who will help me plant the wheat seed?" she asked one springtime.

"Not I," said the dog, the cat and the rat.

"Then I will do it all by myself,"
decided Little Red Hen.

She scattered the seeds in neat rows,
then watered them with her can.

Spring, then summer passed. The crop grew tall and strong.

"Who will help me cut the wheat?" asked Little Red Hen.

"Not I," said the dog, the cat and the rat.

Little Red Hen sighed. "Then I will cut it all by myself," she said.

The animals watched as Little Red Hen cut and harvested the wheat. It was hard, hot work for one.

Little Red Hen put all the sacks of wheat on to her cart and took them to the mill.

"Who will help me grind the wheat?" she asked.

"Not I," said the dog, the cat and the rat.

Little Red Hen frowned. "Then I will grind it all by myself."

Little Red Hen spent many long hours grinding the wheat into flour. She slowly pounded all the grain on her millstone, crushing it into a powder. There were many sacks to get through, but Little Red Hen never complained.

The hours ticked by, but no one offered to help Little Red Hen. After a time she got used to working all by herself.

After a few days, the dog wandered back to the windmill.
The cat and the rat ambled lazily behind.

"What are you doing, Little Red Hen?" the dog asked,
slumping against a grain sack.

"I've not finished grinding the wheat," she answered. "Would
any of you like to help me? There's still plenty to do."

The dog yawned, then stretched out beside the cat. The rat
hopped on to the window ledge.

When they'd all got comfortable, the dog shook his head.

"Not I," he said.

"Not I," said the cat.

"Not I," said the rat.

"Very well," replied Little Red Hen.

She didn't complain. While her friends dozed, Little Red Hen worked on alone. At last, every sack was full of flour.

Little Red Hen dragged the biggest sack of flour into the farmhouse kitchen.

"Who will help me bake the bread?" she asked.

"Not I," said the dog, the cat and the rat.

Little Red Hen slipped on a fresh apron. "Then I will bake it all by myself," she said.

Little Red Hen mixed the flour with other ingredients until it made a yeasty white dough. The animals watched as she kneaded the mixture again and again, but no one offered to help.

Little Red Hen waited for the dough to rise. When it was ready she put it in the oven.

A while later, Little Red Hen took the delicious-smelling
loaf out to cool.

She cut off a thick slice.

"Who will help me eat the bread?" she asked.

The animals scampered up to the table.

"I will," said the dog.

"I will," said the cat.

"I will," said the rat.

Little Red Hen shook her head.

"I planted the seed, cut the wheat, ground the flour and baked the bread all by myself," she explained.

The animals watched eagerly as Little Red Hen
covered the bread in golden butter.
"Now I'm going to eat it all by myself!"

Little Red Hen poured a cup of tea then took a seat at her little table. She ate her way through the loaf until every last crumb was gone.

It was the most delicious meal she had ever had.

GOLDILOCKS AND THE THREE BEARS

A popular nursery tale, first written by the poet Robert Southey

Illustrated by Marina Le Ray

THERE WERE ONCE three bears – a big Daddy Bear,
a middle-sized Mummy Bear and a little Baby Bear.
The bears lived together in a cottage in the woods.
Every morning, Mummy Bear made porridge for breakfast.

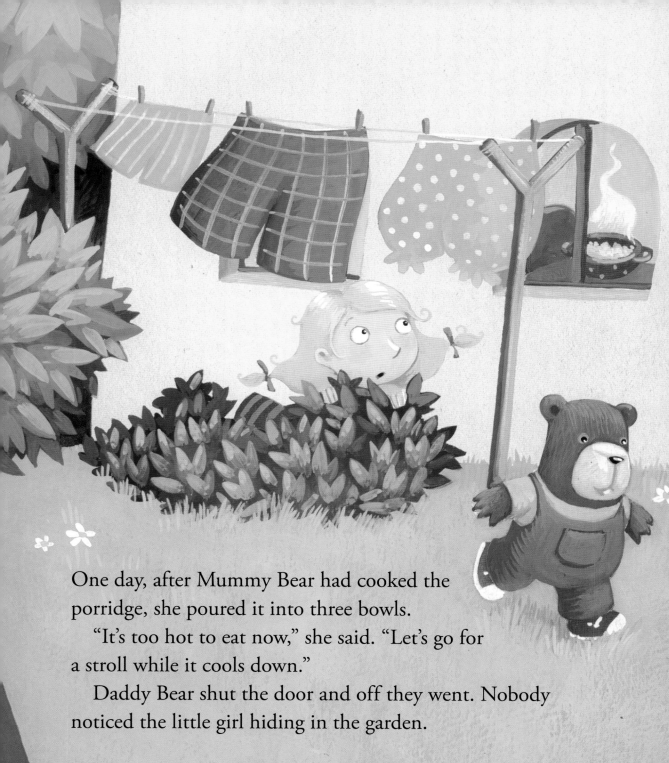

One day, after Mummy Bear had cooked the
porridge, she poured it into three bowls.

"It's too hot to eat now," she said. "Let's go for
a stroll while it cools down."

Daddy Bear shut the door and off they went. Nobody
noticed the little girl hiding in the garden.

The little girl was called Goldilocks. Feeling curious, she lifted the latch on the door and crept inside to look around.

The bears' cottage was warm and cosy. The kitchen dresser was stacked with cheery plates and happy pictures lined the walls.

"Breakfast!" gasped Goldilocks, spying the kitchen table. It had been set for three. There was a big bowl, a middle-sized bowl and a tiny bowl. Each one was full of creamy porridge.

Goldilocks took a mouthful of porridge from the big bowl on the table.

"Oh no!" she cried. "It's much too hot!"

Goldilocks looked over at the middle-sized porridge bowl.

"I'll just try a mouthful," she whispered, hungrily lifting the spoon to her lips.

"Ugh!" spluttered Goldilocks. "It's much too lumpy!"

There was only one bowl left to try. The girl moved round to the little green bowl with bees painted round the edge.

"I'll try a little bit," she decided.

The porridge in the little bowl smelled especially delicious. Goldilocks pulled up a chair and dipped in the spoon lying alongside it.

"Mmmm…!" she beamed. "This porridge is just right."

This breakfast wasn't too hot and it wasn't too lumpy. The little girl liked it so much she ate it all up.

Goldilocks couldn't resist tiptoeing into the bears' cosy living room. Three chairs stood in front of her, arranged in a neat row.

Goldilocks climbed on to the tall chair. "Oh no," she frowned. "This is much too hard!"

The girl walked over to the pink middle-sized chair.
She sank deep into the cushions.

"Definitely not!" said Goldilocks. "This one is much
too soft!"

There was only one chair left to try.

"This chair is just right," she smiled, before the leg broke
with a loud snap!

All this made Goldilocks feel tired. She crept into the bears' bedroom.

"This bed is much too hard," sighed the girl, lying on the big blue bed.

She jumped on to the middle-sized bed next, but it was much too soft.

Finally, Goldilocks rested her head on the littlest bed.

"This bed is just right," she murmured, drifting off to sleep.

Just then, the three bears returned from their walk. Daddy Bear looked round the kitchen.

"Who's been eating my porridge?" he bellowed in a booming voice.

Mummy Bear stared at the splodges on the tablecloth.

"Who's been eating my porridge?" she cried.

Baby Bear ran up to the table and peered into his bowl. His breakfast had disappeared.

"Who's been eating my porridge?" he gasped. "It's all gone!"

Mummy Bear comforted Baby Bear while Daddy Bear strode into the living room.

"Who's been sitting in my chair?" growled Daddy Bear, getting even more cross.

Mummy Bear spotted her cushions and knitting spread all over the floor.

"Who's been sitting in my chair?" she cried.

Mummy and Daddy Bear turned round to look at Baby Bear.

Baby Bear pointed at his little green seat.

"Who's been sitting in my chair?" he sobbed.
"It's been broken in two!"

Mummy and Daddy Bear marched into the bedroom.

"Who's been sleeping in my bed?" frowned Daddy Bear.

The blankets had been disturbed and a slipper knocked on to the floor.

Mummy Bear took one look at the rumpled blanket before her.

"Who's been sleeping in my bed?" she cried.

Suddenly, Baby Bear tugged at his mother's sleeve.

"Who's sleeping in my bed?" shouted Baby Bear. "Look! She's still here!"

Goldilocks woke up with a start.

"Oh my!" she squealed, running out of the bedroom and down the stairs.

Goldilocks fled out of the door and into the woods. She didn't stop until the cottage was far behind her. The three bears never saw the naughty girl again.

THE UGLY DUCKLING

Based on a story by Hans Christian Andersen

Illustrated by Richard Johnson

ONE FINE DAY a mother duck sat on her nest, waiting for her eggs to hatch.

"When will my babies come?" she wondered. "It can't be long now!"

Sure enough, she soon heard a little pecking sound. Each of her eggs began to crack open.

Six of the ducklings were fluffy and sweet. The duck was delighted.

But one of the ducklings was much larger than the rest. He was gangly and grey. Even his mother thought he was ugly.

The mother duck led her brood to the water's edge. The six yellow ducklings waddled into the pond, splashing and cheeping all the while.

"Those six are such sweet ducklings," said the other ducks and geese. "But who is that ugly creature at the back?"

The awkward grey duckling swam in lonely circles round the pond. No one wanted to play with him and nobody wanted to talk to him. Even his own brothers and sisters turned up their little beaks when he swam by.

Word quickly spread. Soon the poor creature was known only as the Ugly Duckling.

The Ugly Duckling grew a little bigger, but he still looked different from the rest of his family.

"You must leave the pond," said his mother. "You don't fit in here."

The other ducklings snuggled together as he sadly swam away.

The Ugly Duckling walked forlornly
through a farm. He had nowhere to go.
  A cow wandered across the meadow to
take a look at the strange-looking bird.
  "Hello," quacked the Ugly Duckling.
"Can I be your friend?"

The cow looked surprised.

"You are an ugly thing," she replied.

"You don't fit in here."

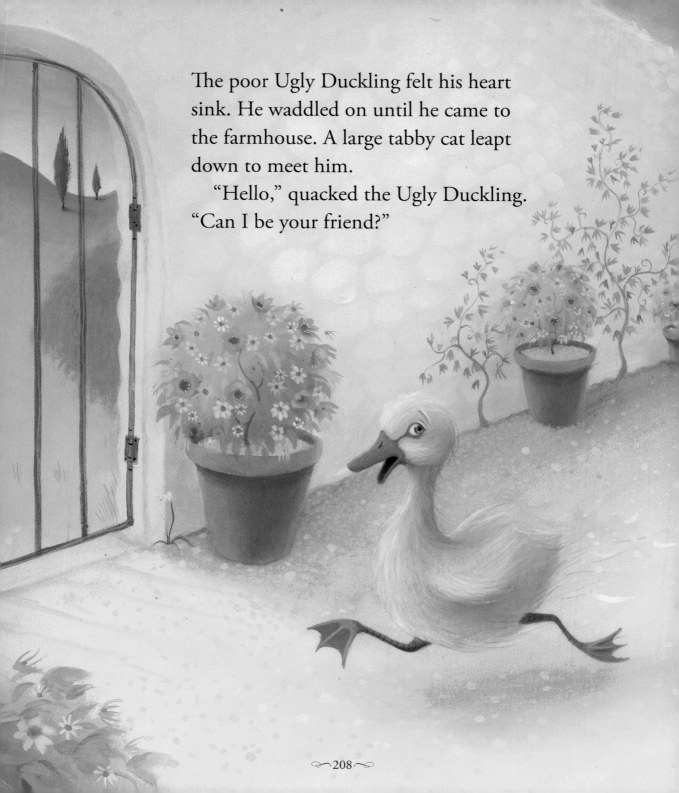

The poor Ugly Duckling felt his heart
sink. He waddled on until he came to
the farmhouse. A large tabby cat leapt
down to meet him.

"Hello," quacked the Ugly Duckling.
"Can I be your friend?"

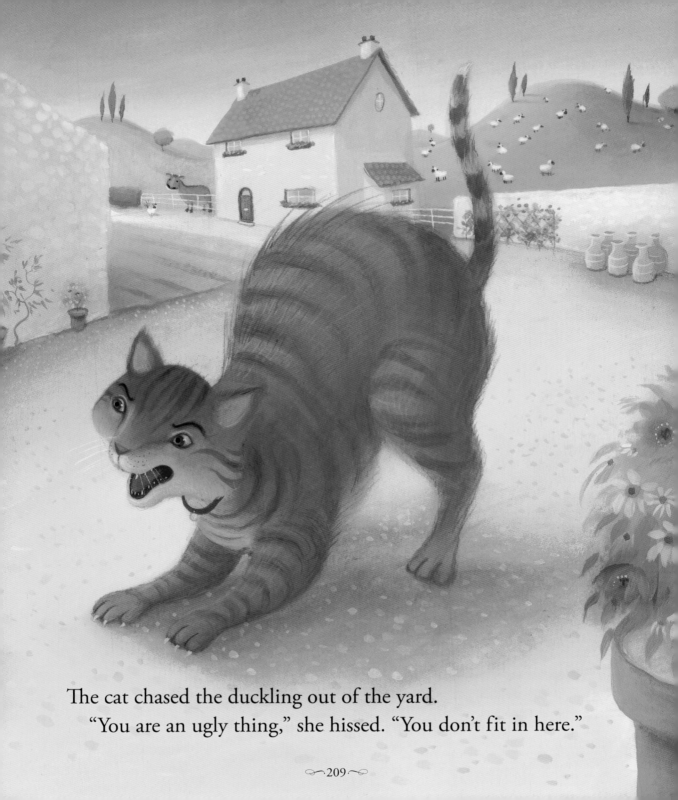

The cat chased the duckling out of the yard.

"You are an ugly thing," she hissed. "You don't fit in here."

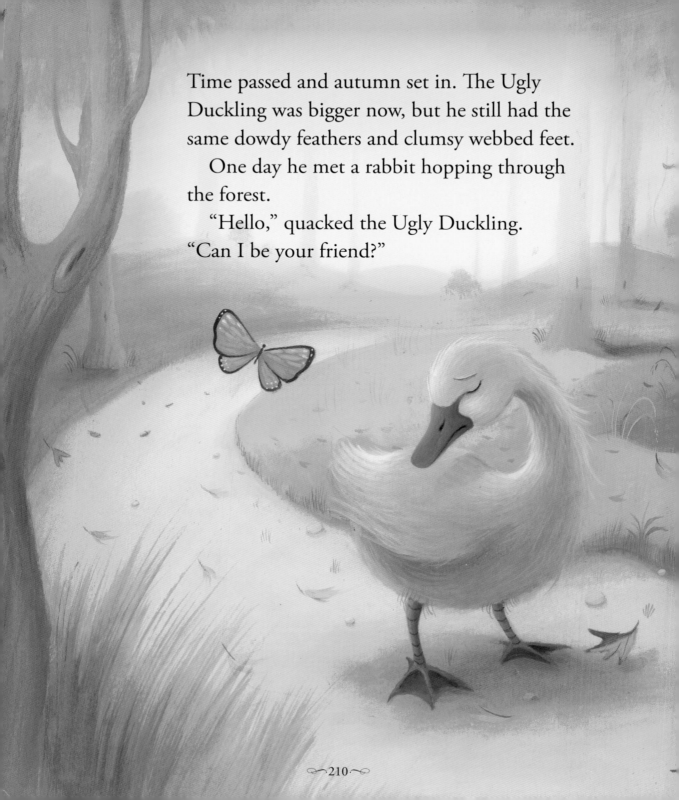

Time passed and autumn set in. The Ugly
Duckling was bigger now, but he still had the
same dowdy feathers and clumsy webbed feet.

One day he met a rabbit hopping through
the forest.

"Hello," quacked the Ugly Duckling.
"Can I be your friend?"

The rabbit stared at the strange grey bird.

"You are an ugly thing," he sniffed. "You don't fit in here."

The days grew shorter and the nights grew colder. The Ugly Duckling waddled all over the land, but nobody wanted to talk to him. He felt happiest curled up alone, hiding himself from the world.

One day a boy discovered the Ugly Duckling trembling behind a fallen tree.

"Hello," quacked the Ugly Duckling. "Can I be your friend?"

The boy wrinkled his nose in horror.

"You are an ugly thing," he scowled. "You don't fit in here."

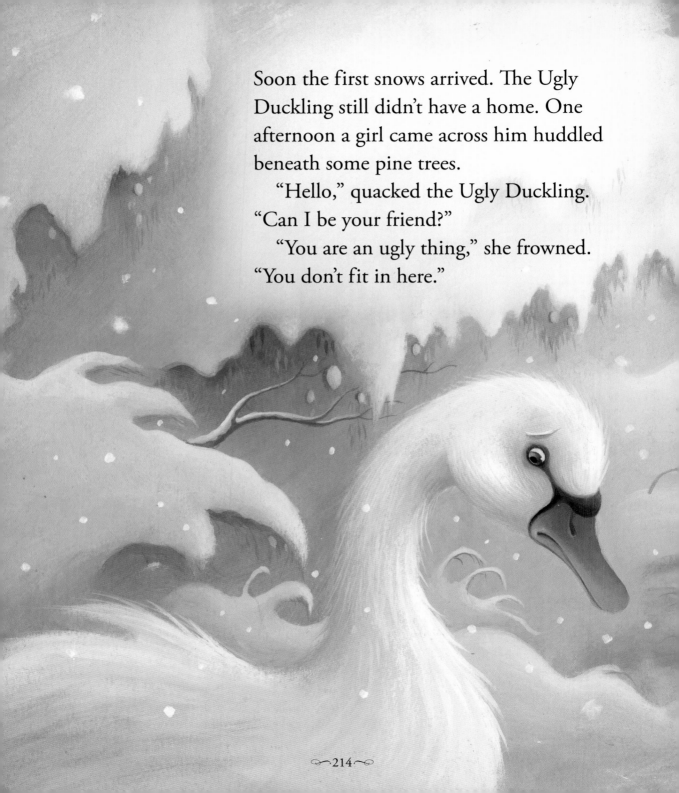

Soon the first snows arrived. The Ugly
Duckling still didn't have a home. One
afternoon a girl came across him huddled
beneath some pine trees.

"Hello," quacked the Ugly Duckling.
"Can I be your friend?"

"You are an ugly thing," she frowned.
"You don't fit in here."

Soon it was winter. With a heavy heart the Ugly Duckling returned to his pond. The frozen waters were cold and lonely, but at least there was nobody there to tease him.

"One day I will fit in," sighed the duckling, looking up to the snowy skies.

The Ugly Duckling made a little bed in the reeds. Here the months passed slowly but peacefully. The humble creature didn't notice his feathers turning milky white. He didn't see how fine and strong his wings had grown.

One day the sun began to melt away the
ice and snow. Spring had arrived at last!

Three stunning swans glided across the
pond. The duckling curved his neck to hide
his ugliness.

"Take a look in the water, friend," cried
the swans.

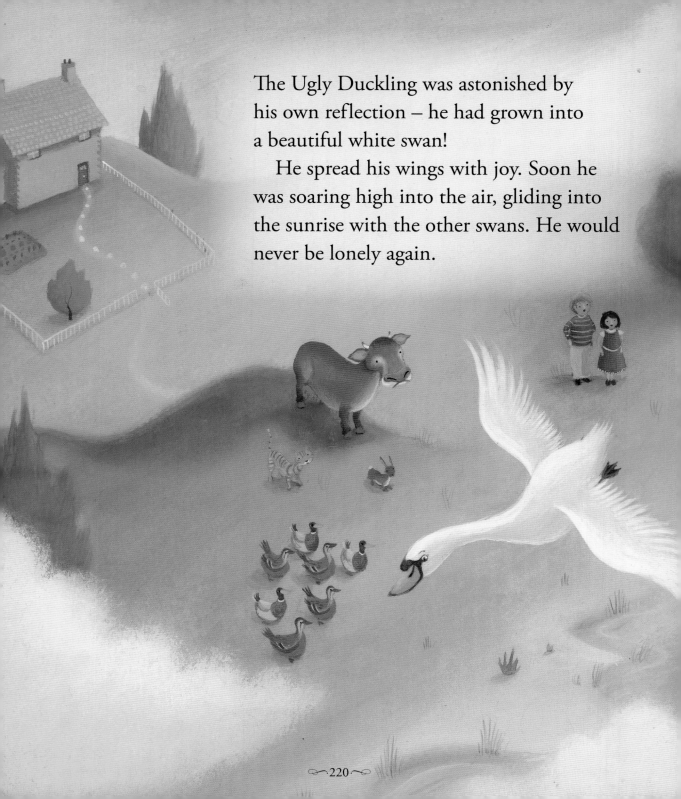

The Ugly Duckling was astonished by
his own reflection – he had grown into
a beautiful white swan!

He spread his wings with joy. Soon he
was soaring high into the air, gliding into
the sunrise with the other swans. He would
never be lonely again.